Winnie-the-Pooh

three books in one

A Very Grand Thing

Based on the stories of A. A. Milne

Halfway between Pooh's house and Piglet's house was a Thoughtful Spot where they met sometimes when they had decided to go and see each other.

Now one autumn morning when the wind had blown all the leaves off the trees in the night, and was trying to blow the branches off, Pooh and Piglet were sitting in the Thoughtful Spot and wondering who to visit.

"Let's go and see *everybody*," said Pooh. "Because when you've been walking in the wind for miles, and you suddenly go into somebody's house, and he says, 'Hallo, Pooh, you're just in time for a little smackerel of something,' and you are, then it's what I call a Friendly Day."

Piglet thought that they ought to have a Reason for going to see everybody, like Looking for Small or Organising an Expotition, if Pooh could think of something.

Pooh could.

"We'll go because it's Thursday," he said, "and we'll go to wish everybody a Very Happy Thursday. Come on, Piglet."

They got up; and when Piglet had sat down again, because he didn't know the wind was so strong, and had been helped up by Pooh, they started off.

They went to Pooh's house first, and luckily Pooh
was at home just as they got there, so he asked them
in, and they had some, and then they went on to
Kanga's house, holding on to each other, and
shouting, "Isn't it?" and "What?" and "I can't hear."
By the time they got to Kanga's house they were so
buffeted that they stayed to lunch. Just at first it
seemed rather cold outside afterwards, so they pushed
on to Rabbit's as quickly as they could.

   "We've come to wish you a
Very Happy Thursday," said
Pooh, when he had gone in and
out once or twice just to make
sure that he *could* get out again.

"Why, what's going to happen on Thursday?" asked Rabbit, and when Pooh had explained, and Rabbit, whose life was made up of Important Things, said, "Oh, I thought you'd

really come about something," they sat down for a little... and by-and-by Pooh and Piglet went on again. The wind was behind them now, so they didn't have to shout.

Christopher Robin was at home by this time, because it was the afternoon, and he was so glad to see them that they stayed there until very nearly tea-time, and then they had a Very Nearly tea, which is one you forget about afterwards, and hurried on to Pooh Corner, so as to see Eeyore before it was too late to have a Proper Tea with Owl.

"Hallo, Eeyore," they called out cheerfully.

"Ah!" said Eeyore. "Lost your way?"

"We just came to see you," said Piglet. "And to see how your house was. Look, Pooh, it's still standing!"

"I know," said Eeyore. "Very odd. Somebody ought to have come down and pushed it over."

"We wondered whether the wind would blow it down," said Pooh.

"Ah, that's why nobody's bothered, I suppose. I thought perhaps they'd forgotten."

Pooh and Piglet shuffled about a little and said, "Well, good-bye, Eeyore," as lingeringly as they could, but they had a long way to go, and wanted to be getting on to Owl's house.

The wind was against them now, and Piglet's ears streamed behind him like banners as he fought his way along, and it seemed hours before he got them

into the shelter of the Hundred Acre Wood and they stood up straight again, to listen, a little nervously, to the roaring of the gale among the tree-tops.

"Supposing a tree fell down, Pooh, when we were underneath it?"

"Supposing it didn't," said Pooh after careful thought.

Piglet was comforted by this, and in a little while they were knocking and ringing very cheerfully at Owl's door.

"Hallo, Owl," said Pooh. "I hope we're not too late for – I mean, how are you, Owl? Piglet and I just came to see how you were because it's Thursday."

"Sit down, Pooh, sit down, Piglet," said Owl kindly. "Make yourselves comfortable."

They thanked him, and made themselves as comfortable as they could.

"Because, you see, Owl," said Pooh, "we've been hurrying, so as to be in time for – so as to see you before we went away again."

Owl nodded solemnly.

"Correct me if I am wrong," he said, "but am I right in supposing that it is a very Blusterous day outside?"

"Very," said Piglet, who was quietly thawing his ears, and wishing that he was safely back in his own house.

"I thought so," said Owl. "It was on just such a blusterous day as this that my Uncle Robert, a portrait of whom you see upon the wall on your right, Piglet, while returning in the late forenoon from a – What's that?"

There was a loud cracking noise.

"Look out!" cried Pooh. "Mind the clock! Out of the way, Piglet! Piglet, I'm falling on you!"

"Help!" cried Piglet.

Pooh's side of the room was slowly tilting upwards and his chair began sliding down on Piglet's. The clock slithered gently along the mantel-piece, collecting vases on the way, until they all crashed together on to what had once been the floor, but was now trying to see what it looked like as a wall. Uncle Robert, who was going to be the new hearthrug, and was bringing the rest of his wall with him as carpet, met Piglet's chair just as Piglet was expecting to leave it, and for a little while it became very difficult to remember which was really the north. Then there was another loud crack...

Owl's room collected itself
feverishly ... and there was silence.
   In a corner of the room, the table-
cloth began to wriggle.

   Then it wrapped itself into a ball
and rolled across the room.
   Then it jumped up and down once
or twice, and put out two ears.

It rolled across the room again, and unwound itself.

"Pooh," said Piglet nervously.

"Yes?" said one of the chairs.

"Where are we?"

"I'm not quite sure," said the chair.

"Are we – are we in Owl's House?"

"I think so, because we were just going to have tea, and we hadn't had it."

"Oh!" said Piglet. "Well, did Owl *always* have a letter-box in his ceiling?"

"Has he?"

"Yes, look."

"I can't," said Pooh. "I'm face downwards under something, and that, Piglet, is a very bad position for looking at ceilings."

"Well, he has, Pooh."

"Perhaps he's changed it," said Pooh. "Just for a change."

There was a disturbance behind the table in the other corner of the room, and Owl was with them again.

"Ah, Piglet," said Owl, looking very much annoyed; "where's Pooh?"

"I'm not quite sure," said Pooh.

Owl turned at his voice, and frowned at as much of Pooh as he could see.

"Pooh," said Owl severely, "did *you* do that?"

"No," said Pooh humbly. "I don't *think* so."

"Then who did?"

"I think it was the wind," said Piglet. "I think your house has blown down."

"Oh, is that it? I thought it was Pooh."

"No," said Pooh.

"If it was the wind," said Owl, considering the matter, "then it wasn't Pooh's fault. No blame can be attached to him."

With these kind words Owl and Piglet pushed and pulled at the arm-chair, and in a little while Pooh came out from underneath, and was able to look round him again.

"Well!" said Owl. "This is a nice state of things! What are we going to do, Pooh?"

"Can you think of anything?" asked Piglet.

"Because," said Owl, "we can't go out by what used to be the front door. Something's fallen on it."

"But how else *can* you go out?" asked Piglet anxiously.

"That is the Problem, Piglet, to which I am asking Pooh to give his mind."

Pooh sat on the floor which had once been a wall, and gazed up at the ceiling which had once been another wall, with a front door in it which had once been a front door, and tried to give his mind to it.

"Could you fly up to the letter-box with Piglet on your back?" he asked.

"No," said Piglet quickly. "He couldn't."

"Because you see, Owl, if we could get Piglet into the letter-box, he might squeeze through the place where the letters come, and climb down the tree and run for help."

Owl explained that he didn't have the Necessary Dorsal Muscles, and Piglet said, "Then we'd better think of something else," and began to at once.

But Pooh's mind had gone back to the day when he had saved Piglet from the flood, and everybody had admired him so much; and as that didn't often happen, he thought he would like it to happen again. And suddenly, just as it had come before, an idea came to him.

"Owl," said Pooh. "I have thought of something."

"Astute and Helpful Bear," said Owl.

Pooh looked proud at being called a stout and helpful bear, and said modestly that he just happened to think of it.

You tied a piece of string to Piglet, and you flew up to the letter-box, with the other end in your beak, and you pushed it through the wire and brought it down to the floor, and you and Pooh pulled hard at this end, and Piglet went slowly up at the other end. And there you were.

"And there Piglet is," said Owl. "If the string doesn't break."

"Supposing it does?" asked Piglet, really wanting to know.

"It won't break," whispered Pooh comfortingly, "because you're a Small Animal, and I'll stand underneath, and if you save us all, it will be a Very Grand Thing to talk about afterwards."

Piglet felt much better after this, and when everything was ready, and he found himself slowly going up to the ceiling, he was so proud that he would have called out "Look at me!" if he hadn't been afraid that Pooh and Owl would let go of their end of the string and look at him.

"Up we go!" said Pooh cheerfully.

"The ascent is proceeding as expected," said Owl helpfully. Soon it was over. Piglet opened the letter-box, climbed in and squeezed out to the other side.

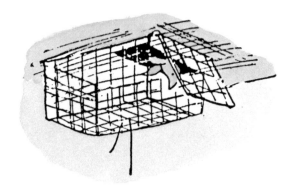

Happy and excited he turned round to squeak a last message to the prisoners.

"It's all right," he called through the letter-box. "Your tree is blown right over, Owl, and there's a branch across the door, but Christopher Robin and I will be back in about half an hour. Good-bye, Pooh!" And without waiting to hear Pooh's answering "Good-bye, and thank you, Piglet," he was off.

"Half an hour," said Owl, settling himself comfortably. "That will just give me time to finish that story I was telling you about my Uncle Robert – a portrait of whom you see underneath you. Now let me see, where was I? Oh, yes. It was on just such a blusterous day as this that my Uncle Robert —"

Pooh closed his eyes.

Piglet is Rescued

It rained and it rained and it rained. Piglet told himself that never in all his life, never had he seen so much rain. Days and days and days.

"If only," he thought, as he looked out of the window, "I had been in Pooh's house, or Christopher Robin's house, or Rabbit's house when it began to rain, then I should have had Company all this time, instead of being here all alone, with nothing to do except wonder when it will stop."

And he imagined himself
with Pooh, saying, "Did you
ever see such rain, Pooh?"
and Pooh saying,
"Isn't it *awful*, Piglet?"

It would have been jolly to talk like this, and really, it wasn't
much good having anything exciting like floods, if you couldn't
share them with somebody.

For it was rather exciting. The little dry ditches in which Piglet had nosed about so often had become streams, the little streams across which he had splashed were rivers, and the river, between whose steep banks they had played so happily, had sprawled out of its own bed and was taking up so much room everywhere, that Piglet was beginning to wonder whether it would be coming into *his* bed soon.

"It's a little Anxious," he said to himself, "to be a Very Small Animal Entirely Surrounded by Water. And I can't do *anything*."

It went on raining, and every day the water got a little higher, until now it was nearly up to Piglet's window...and he hadn't done anything.

Then suddenly he remembered a story which Christopher Robin had told him about a man on a desert island who had written something in a bottle and thrown it into the sea; and Piglet thought that if he wrote something in a bottle and threw it in the water, perhaps somebody would come and rescue *him!*

He left the window and began to search the house, and at last he found a pencil and a small piece of dry paper, and a bottle with a cork to it. And he wrote on one side of the paper:

 HELP!
PIGLIT (ME)

and on the other side:

IT'S ME PIGLIT, HELP HELP!

Then he put the paper in the bottle, and he threw the bottle as far as he could throw and he watched it floating slowly away in the distance.

When the rain began Pooh was asleep. It rained, and it rained, and it rained, and he slept, and he slept, and he slept. He had had a tiring day. You remember how he discovered the North Pole; well, he was so proud of this that he asked Christopher Robin if there were any other Poles such as a Bear of Little Brain might discover.

"There's a South Pole," said Christopher Robin, "and I expect there's an East Pole and a West Pole, though people don't like talking about them."

Then suddenly he was dreaming. He was at the East Pole, and it was a very cold pole with snow and ice all over it. He had found a beehive to sleep in, but there wasn't room for his legs, so he had left them outside. And Wild Woozles, such as inhabit the East Pole, came and nibbled all the fur off his legs to make Nests for their Young. And the more they nibbled, the colder his legs got, until suddenly he woke up with an *Ow!* – and there he was, sitting in his chair with his feet in the water, and water all round him!

He splashed to his door and looked out...

"This is Serious," said Pooh. "I must have an Escape."

So he took his largest pot of honey and escaped with it to a broad branch of his tree, well above the water, and then he climbed down again and escaped with another pot...and when the whole Escape was finished, there was Pooh sitting on his branch, dangling his legs, and there, beside him, were ten pots of honey...

Two days later, there was Pooh, sitting on his branch, dangling his legs, and there beside him, were four pots of honey.
Three days later, there was Pooh, sitting on his branch, dangling his legs, and there beside him, was one pot of honey.
Four days later, there was Pooh...

And it was on the morning of the fourth day that Piglet's bottle come floating past him, and with one loud cry of "Honey!" Pooh plunged into the water, seized the bottle, and struggled back to his tree again.

"Bother!" said Pooh, as he opened it. "All that wet for nothing. What's that bit of paper doing?"

He took it out and looked.

"It's a Missage," he said to himself, "and I can't read it. I must find Christopher Robin or Owl or Piglet, and they will tell me what this missage means. Only I can't swim. Bother!"

Then he had an idea. He said to himself:

"If a bottle can float, then a jar can float, and if a jar floats, I can sit on the top of it, if it's a very big jar."

So he took his biggest jar, and corked it up.

"All boats have to have a name," he said, "so I shall call mine *The Floating Bear*." And with these words he dropped his boat into the water and jumped in after it.

Christopher Robin lived at the very top of the Forest. It rained, and it rained, and it rained, but the water couldn't come up to *his* house. It was rather jolly to look down into the valleys and see the water all round him, but it rained so hard that he stayed indoors most of the time, and thought about things.

Every morning he went out with his umbrella and put a stick in the place where the water came up to, and every next morning he went out and couldn't see his stick any more, so he put another stick in the place where the water came up to. On the morning of the fifth day he saw the water all round him, and knew that for the first time in his life he was on a real island.

It was on this morning that Owl came flying over the water to say "How do you do?" to his friend Christopher Robin.

"I say, Owl," said Christopher Robin, "isn't this fun? I'm on an island!"

"The atmospheric conditions have been very unfavourable lately," said Owl.

"The what?"

"It has been raining," Owl explained.

"Yes," said Christopher Robin. "It has. Have you seen Pooh?"

"Here I am," said a growly voice behind him.

"Pooh!"

They rushed into each other's arms.

"How did you get here, Pooh?" asked Christopher Robin.

"On my boat," said Pooh proudly. "I had a Very Important Missage sent me in a bottle, and owing to having got some water in my eyes, I couldn't read it, so I brought it to you. On my boat."

With these proud words he gave Christopher Robin the missage.

"But it's from Piglet!" cried Christopher Robin when he had read it. "We must rescue him at once! Owl, could you rescue him on your back?"

"I don't think so," said Owl.

"Then would you fly to him at once and say the Rescue is Coming? And Pooh and I will think of a Rescue and come as quick as ever we can."

Owl, speechless for once, flew off.

"Now then, Pooh," said Christopher Robin, "where's your boat?"

"There!" said Pooh, pointing proudly to *The Floating Bear*.

It wasn't what Christopher Robin expected, and the more he looked at it, the more he thought what a Brave and Clever Bear Pooh was. Pooh looked modestly down his nose and tried to pretend he wasn't.

"But it's too small for two of us," said Christopher Robin sadly.

"Three of us with Piglet."

"That makes it smaller still. Oh, Pooh Bear, what shall we do?"

And then this Bear, Pooh Bear, said something so clever that Christopher Robin could only look at him with mouth open and eyes staring. "We might go in your umbrella," said Pooh.

For suddenly Christopher Robin saw that they might. He opened his umbrella and put it point downwards in the water. It floated but wobbled. Pooh got in.

He was just beginning to say that it was all right now, when he found that it wasn't. Then Christopher Robin got in, and it wobbled no longer.

You can imagine Piglet's joy when at last he saw the good ship *Brain of Pooh* (*Captain*, C. Robin; *1st Mate*, P. Bear), coming over the sea to rescue him...

And as that is really the end of the story, I think I shall stop there.

A Grand Party for Pooh

One day, when the sun had come back over the Forest, and all the streams of the Forest were tinkling happily to find themselves their own pretty shape again, the little pools lay dreaming of the life they had seen and the big things they had done. In the warmth and quiet of the Forest, wood-pigeons were complaining gently to themselves in their lazy comfortable way that it was the other fellow's fault, but it didn't matter very much. On such a day as this Christopher Robin whistled in a special way he had, and Owl came flying out of the Hundred Acre Wood to see what was wanted.

"Owl," said Christopher Robin, "I am going to give a party."

"You are, are you?" said Owl.

"And it's to be a special sort of party, because it's because of what Pooh did when he did what he did to save Piglet from the flood."

"Oh, that's what it's for, is it?" said Owl, helpfully.

"Yes, so will you tell Pooh as quickly as you can, and all the others, because it will be tomorrow?"

"Oh, it will, will it?" said Owl, still being as helpful as possible.

"So will you go and tell them, Owl?"

Owl tried to think of something wise to say, but he couldn't, so he flew off to tell the others. And the first person he told was Pooh.

"Pooh," he said. "Christopher Robin is giving a party."

"Oh!" said Pooh. And then seeing that Owl expected him to say something else, he said, "Will there be those little cake things with pink sugar icing?"

Owl felt that it was rather beneath him to talk about little cake things with pink sugar icing, so he told Pooh exactly what Christopher Robin had said, and flew off to Eeyore.

"A party for Me?" thought Pooh to himself. "How grand!" And he began to wonder if all the other animals would know that it was a special Pooh Party, and if Christopher Robin had told them about *The Floating Bear* and the *Brain of Pooh* and all the wonderful ships he had invented and sailed on.

While this was going on inside him, Owl was talking to Eeyore.

"Eeyore," said Owl, "Christopher Robin is giving a party."

"Very interesting," said Eeyore. "I suppose they will be sending me down the odd bits which got trodden on. Kind and Thoughtful. Not at all, don't mention it."

"There is an Invitation for you."

"What's that like?"

"An Invitation!"

"Yes, I heard you. Who dropped it?"

"This isn't anything to eat, it's asking you to the party. Tomorrow."

Eeyore shook his head slowly.

"You mean Piglet. The little fellow with the excited ears. That's Piglet. I'll tell him."

"No, no," said Owl, getting quite fussy. "It's you!"

"Are you sure?"

"Of course I'm sure. Christopher Robin said 'All of them! Tell all of them.'"

"All of them, except Eeyore?"

"All of them," said Owl sulkily.

"Ah!" said Eeyore. "A mistake, no doubt, but still, I shall come. Only don't blame *me* if it rains."

But it didn't rain. Christopher Robin had made a long table out of some long pieces of wood, and they all sat round it. Christopher Robin sat at one end, and Pooh sat at the other, and between them on one side were Owl and Eeyore and Piglet, and between them on the other side were Rabbit, and Roo and Kanga. It was the first party to which Roo had ever been, and he was very excited. As soon as ever they had sat down he began to talk.

"Hallo, Pooh!" he squeaked.

"Hallo, Roo!" said Pooh.

Roo jumped up and down in his seat for a little while and then began again.

"Hallo, Piglet!" he squeaked.

Piglet waved a paw at him, being too busy to say anything.

"Hallo, Eeyore!" said Roo.

Eeyore nodded gloomily at him. "It will rain soon, you see if it doesn't," he said.

Roo looked to see if it didn't, and it didn't, so he said "Hallo, Owl" – and Owl said "Hallo, my little fellow," in a kindly way, and went on talking to Christopher Robin, and Kanga said to Roo, "Drink up your milk first, dear, and talk afterwards." So Roo, who was drinking his milk, tried to say that he could do both at once … and had to be patted on the back and dried for quite a long time afterwards.

When they had all nearly eaten enough,
Christopher Robin banged on the table with
his spoon, and everybody stopped talking and
was very silent.

"This party," said Christopher Robin, "is a party because of what someone did, and we all know who it was, and it's his party, because of what he did, and I've got a present for him and here it is." Then he felt about a little and whispered, "Where is it?"

While he was looking, Eeyore coughed in an impressive way and began to speak.

"Friends," he said, "it is a great pleasure, or perhaps I had better say it has been a pleasure so far, to see you at my party. What I did was nothing. Any of you – except Rabbit and Owl and Kanga – would have done the same. Oh, and Pooh. My remarks do not, of course, apply to Piglet and Roo, because they are too small. Any of you would have done the same. But it just happened to be Me. It was not, I need hardly say, with an idea of getting what Christopher Robin is looking for now" – and he put his front leg to his mouth and said in a loud whisper, "Try under the table" – "that I did what I did – because I feel that we should all do what we can to help. I feel that we should all –"

"What's Eeyore talking about?" Piglet whispered to Pooh.

"I don't know," said Pooh rather dolefully.

"I thought this was *your* party."

"I thought it was *once*. But I suppose it isn't."

"I'd sooner it was yours than Eeyore's," said Piglet.

"So would I," said Pooh.

"AS – I – WAS – SAYING," said Eeyore loudly and sternly, "as I was saying when I was interrupted by various Loud Sounds, I feel that –"

"Here it is!" cried Christopher Robin excitedly. "Pass it down to silly old Pooh. It's for Pooh."

"For Pooh?" said Eeyore.

"Of course it is. The best bear in all the world."

"I might have known," said Eeyore. "After all, one can't complain. I have my friends. Somebody spoke to me only yesterday."

Nobody was listening, for they were all saying, "Open it, Pooh." And of course Pooh was opening it as quickly as ever he could, but without cutting the string, because you never know when a bit of string might be Useful. At last it was undone.

When Pooh saw what it was, he nearly fell down, he was so pleased. It was a Special Pencil Case. There were pencils in it marked 'B' for Bear, and pencils marked 'HB' for Helping Bear, and pencils marked 'BB' for Brave Bear.

There was a knife for sharpening the pencils, and indiarubber for rubbing out anything which you had spelt wrong, and a ruler for ruling lines for the words to walk on, and inches marked on the ruler in case you wanted to know how many inches anything was, and Blue Pencils and Red Pencils and Green Pencils for saying special things in blue and red and green. And all these lovely things were in little pockets of their own in a Special Case which shut with a click when you clicked it. And they were all for Pooh.

"Oh!" said Pooh.

"Oh, Pooh!" said everybody else except Eeyore.

"Thank you," growled Pooh.

Later on, when they had all said "Goodbye" and "Thank you" to Christopher Robin, Pooh and Piglet walked home thoughtfully together in the golden evening, and for a long time they were silent.

"When you wake up in the morning, Pooh," said Piglet at last, "what's the first thing you say to yourself?"

"What's for breakfast?" said Pooh. "What do *you*, say, Piglet?"

"I say, I wonder what's going to happen exciting *today*?" said Piglet.

Pooh nodded thoughtfully.

"It's the same thing," he said.